THE DISAPPEARANCE OF JANUARY DUST

and Other Stories

Collins

Contents

Unit 14

Core: Thank Goodness for Boxing 6

Core: Best Friends Forever................... 24

Challenge: The Disappearance of
January Dust 42

Challenge: Youth Action for Change 60

Thank Goodness for Boxing

Written by Oliver Sykes

Illustrated by Elijah Vardo

This is the author's true story. It contains themes including divorce, money problems and bullying.

When I was as young as 5 years old, my siblings and I would take it in turns to put on a pair of boxing gloves. Our dad would then skip about the living room and call out combinations of boxing moves for us to follow. He'd wear special pads on both hands and we'd hit them as hard as we could, with ferocious intent.

"Jab!" he'd yell.

BANG!

"One-two!"

BANG! BANG!

I was the third oldest child, so I was the third in line to have a go. I remember burning with impatience as I waited for my two older brothers to finish their turns.

When it was eventually my go, I would shake with elation, like an over-excited puppy. I always felt that same burst of energy – that pure joy – as I wildly swung my gloved fists for those precious few minutes. No matter how many turns I had, punching those pads always left me feeling hungry for more.

Every weekend, our whole family would squeeze into the living room in the evening to watch old boxing matches on our little box-shaped TV. Muhammad Ali was my dad's hero, and he quickly became mine, too. I loved watching the build-up to his fights, just as much as I loved his sensational skills in the boxing ring. The whole thing felt like a passionate performance, almost like poetry.

When I was 8 years old, our mum made the decision to leave one day and didn't come back. This left our family without much money. My dad had to care for my three brothers, two sisters and me all by himself. He had gone through a similar situation when he was my age. His parents had split up, and he was picked on for it at school by some nasty kids. So, he made it his mission to not let that happen to me or my siblings.

I didn't feel sad or abandoned when my mum left (although I did experience those feelings when I was older). At the time, my main emotion was anger. I also felt relieved that she walked out. The thing was, I never had a close relationship with my mum. Far from it. I didn't feel like she cared about me or showed me much love and affection, especially compared to how she acted with my siblings. I often felt like I was the one who got blamed if something went wrong. She always seemed so much stricter with me than anyone else.

After she left, everything changed. When I was between 9 and 12 years old, my dad started to drive me and my siblings to Buxton Boxing Club three times a week. It was here that I'd train for 90 minutes like a warrior. Boxing was a distraction from everything that had happened at home. Those sessions at the club helped me let go of my bottled-up anger and frustration.

At the gym, I met other kids like me and became more aware of my situation and who I really was. I was a young boy without a mother. My family didn't have much money. But I had hope for a better life. I thought boxing could be our way out. I'd work hard, be successful and earn a lot of money to help us.

When I was 13 years old, I had my first boxing match. I'll never forget how scared I was before the fight. My guts churned. My arms felt as light as feathers. I was so dizzy. But with my dad by my side, I kept my cool. With great determination, I faced my fears and won! From that day on, boxing was my main passion. I was prepared to make it my whole life.

At 16 years old, I was so excited about my future.
I was a talented boxer with bags of ambition.
I showed my potential by winning lots of fights.
I told myself that I was going to be a star.

My dad was my coach. Our shared mission was to win the national youth championships, then to get to the Olympics. Finally, I'd turn professional and we would work together to win a world title.

But in just one night, that dream of ours was taken away.

I was having a well-deserved night off from my usual training sessions to ride my BMX. I was rolling around the skate park, when there was an explosion of glass right in front of me. I was showered with shards of a broken bottle. I fell off my bike and hit the ground hard. I lay there, shocked and motionless.

Next thing I knew, I was being attacked. There wasn't time to think, only to feel, and all I could feel were jolts of excruciating pain.

When I opened my eyes, I saw a boy from the year above me at school. He glared at me and pinned down my arm as his friend hurt my hand. It was my right hand: my main boxing hand.

The next morning, I looked at my reflection in the bathroom mirror and realised my boxing dreams were over. My right hand was badly hurt and would never be the same again. I was devastated. It was as if I was living in a nightmare.

In that moment, the thing I wanted the most in the world was my mum's love and compassion. At the time, I wouldn't dare to admit that out loud. But deep down, I needed her to wrap her arms around me, to hold me tight and to tell me that everything was going to be OK.

I may not have had my mum, but I did have my dad. Men of his generation didn't do physical affection like hugs. But he comforted me as best he could, in his own way. He encouraged me to dust myself off and focus on my education.

So, I did. In my school years, storytelling soon replaced boxing as my biggest passion. This passion persevered through college, university and into the world of work.

At the time of writing this, I am 36 years old, and I am very proud to be a successful author, poet, writer and performer. Not only that, but boxing has found its way back to me as an inspiration for my creative projects.

What I've come to realise is that my relationship with boxing extends far beyond the ring. It is a part of my family. It runs deep in my blood. That means it's always with me.

No matter how many times life has knocked me down, boxing has always been there to help me get back up. It united me, my dad and my siblings when we needed it most. It gave me friends when I felt alone. It helped build my confidence when I had none. So, that's why I say, "Thank goodness for boxing!"

Did you know? One of Muhammad Ali's children, Laila Ali, was also a boxer!

Early life

Laila Ali was born on 30th December 1977 in the United States. Her father (Muhammad) was a boxer, and her mother (Veronica) was an actress and model.

Her parents divorced when she was nine years old and her turbulent childhood led to her living in a home for girls.

She graduated from college with a business degree and owned her own nail salon before she began boxing.

Boxing career

Between 1999 and 2007, Laila Ali had a perfect boxing record: 24 wins, 0 losses and 21 knockouts. She won multiple world titles.

She was an undefeated four-time world champion boxer! Many people believe Laila Ali is one of the greatest professional boxers of all time.

Best Friends Forever

Written by Kereen Getten

Illustrated by Daniella Gyambibi-Peters

AMY'S DIARY

Dear Diary,

Ten months ago, I moved home to go to a specialist drama school in London. I moved with my family but left my friends behind. I don't want you to think I'm complaining, I'm not. I've wanted this my entire life – performing is my passion. It's just, I miss my best friends, Justin and Cain. We all have our birthdays in July and our tradition is to do something fun, all together, but this year is different. Mine was on 1st July and I spent it without them, though Mum and Dad did take me to the West End to see my favourite show. It's not the same though, especially as it's so hard to make friends in the city.

JUSTIN'S BLOG

It's day 181 of living at the end of the world. Never in my life did I think I'd live on a farm on a Scottish island. When Mum first mentioned that we'd be moving to a slower life, I thought she meant Spain. I'm trying to make the most of it and socialise though. Sam from next door showed us how to shear sheep and, let me tell you, it was traumatising!

Anyway, tomorrow we're going into the village. Sam says they have the best fish and chips for miles. I'll be the judge of that.

CAIN

Cain follows the crowd out of the school gates. It is still strange not seeing Amy and Justin waiting for him. They would usually walk home together. He pulls out his phone and sends a message to the group chat.

July Crew

Cain: Remember when Justin fainted in Geography?

Amy: We got such a scare!

Justin: Why would you bring that up?

Cain: I miss you that's all.

Justin: Happy birthday!

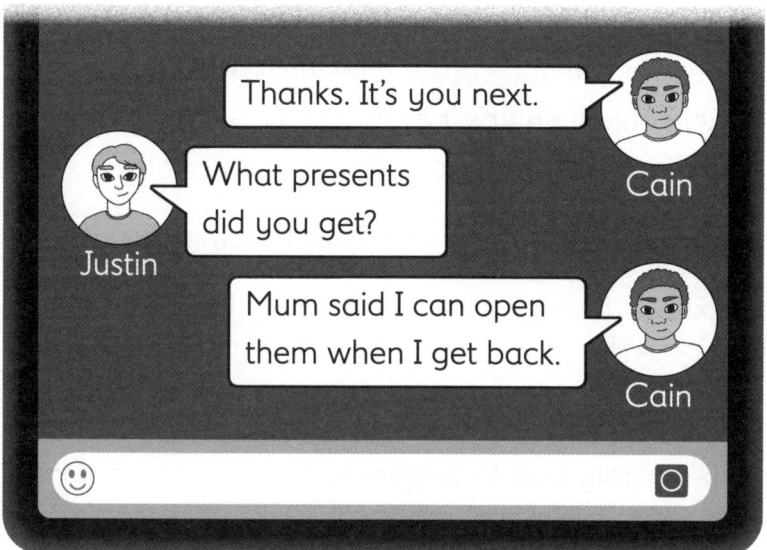

Cain slips his phone in his pocket and hurries home.

His mum is already waiting at the door, with an excited expression. She hugs him tightly. "Happy birthday!"

"Thanks, Mum," he says, dropping his bag on the floor. She ushers him into the living room where there's a chocolate cake surrounded by birthday cards and presents.

She hands him a card. "Mine, first," she says excitedly. Cain rips it open and two tickets fall to the floor. He picks them up and stares at them.

"Concert tickets?" he asks in disbelief.

"I know you've wanted to see Belly Up for a long time."

Cain throws his arms around her. "Thanks, Mum." He's hardly able to believe it.

"I'm conscious that there are only two tickets though," she adds. "I know your birthday celebrations are usually with Amy and Justin, and this could be a perfect reunion for you all, but I couldn't afford three tickets. So, you'll have to make a decision."

"It's OK, Mum," he says.

"Who will you take?" she asks him.

Cain stares at the tickets, knowing one of his friends will be disappointed.

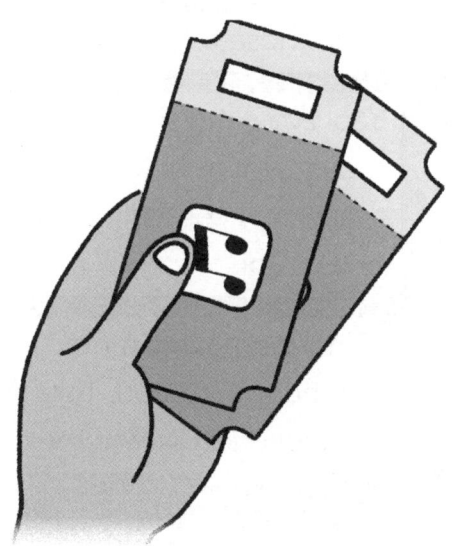

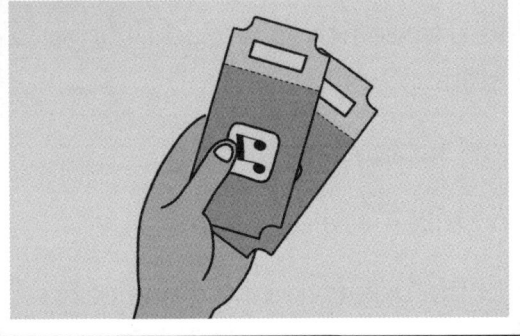

JUSTIN

Justin throws his phone on the bed and drags his feet downstairs where Penny the sheep dog jumps up to get attention.

"I'm taking Penny for a walk," he calls through to the living room.

His mum appears in the hall wiping her hands on a kitchen towel. "You seem sad," she says, with a concerned expression. "What happened?"

Justin lifts his eyes to look at her. "Belly Up are playing in London and Cain has tickets for him and Amy."

She frowns. "Mmm, your favourite band, yes I heard. I know your birthday is coming up, but we're not in a financial position to get you a ticket. I'm sorry, Justin."

Justin nods, clipping the lead onto Penny's collar. "That's alright," he says quietly, and heads outside.

AMY

Amy spots Bianca in the corridor and runs to catch up with her. "Bianca!"

Bianca turns to look at her.

"Amy," Amy says pointing to herself. "We're in the same acting class. We're doing *Romeo and Juliet* together – we auditioned on the same day."

Bianca stares at her blankly.

Amy clears her throat. "Never mind, one of my best friends just had their birthday and they got two tickets to see Belly Up, and my other best friend wants me to have the ticket, but he lives in the middle of nowhere and it's his birthday next week because we all have birthdays in the same month ..."

"What's your point?" Bianca interrupts impatiently.

Amy takes a breath. "Your dad, he owns a record company, doesn't he?"

"Yes, and?"

Amy twists her fingers nervously. "Could you maybe see if he can get a ticket for my friend? I heard you telling Omar the other day that you had tickets."

Bianca looks her over. "I might potentially have a spare ticket," she says. "But, you're not the only one who wants it, so make me an offer."

Amy thinks. "I don't have money but maybe I can help you with your lines for the play?"

Bianca's eyes light up. "You would do that?"

Amy nods, "I know every word in the play."

Bianca sighs with relief. "I'm so bad at remembering lines! It goes in one ear and out the other."

Amy beams. "I'll have you memorising it in no time. I have this special method I use. I'll share it with you."

MUSIC MONTHLY

Belly Up gets 5-stars!

Music sensations Belly Up filled a huge London stadium last night with their latest tour.

Fans travelled far and wide to see them perform. Here is what they had to say:

Incredible musicians! It was such a great concert!

We were so lucky to get tickets! Belly Up are a really special band!

They play with such passion!

We're already impatient for their next performance!

It was a mission to get here all the way from Scotland but totally worth it!

The Disappearance of January Dust

Written by Kereen Getten

Illustrated by Wan Norazura

I met January Dust on my first day at Blackthorn Boarding School. She sat next to me in assembly, her uniform perfectly pressed and her long, sleek, black ponytail trailing down her back.

"I'm January," she said. Her eyes had a bright and hopeful expression.

"Kacey," I replied.

From that day on, we were great friends.

Three weeks into term, January jumped on my bed with an excited squeal. "You won't believe what just happened to me!"

I looked up from my book. "You stopped an alien invasion?"

January rolled her eyes. "I met Teresa Campbell! She runs the Midnight Club. It's the most exclusive secret society at Blackthorn!"

Teresa was the kind of person who liked to be the centre of attention.

"She gave me this invitation. It's for the initiation to the Midnight Club! Apparently, it's like an audition for their special society," January continued.

I closed my book and sat up. "I told you, Teresa is bad news."

TOP SECRET

The Midnight Club

Initiation this Sunday

Meet by the art hut at 7 p.m.

January's face fell. "But I want to experience everything here at Blackthorn," she said, passionately. "I said I'd go but that you had to come with me, and she agreed."

I was always afraid someone would take advantage of January. She was so trusting and keen to be accepted. Unlike me. I was naturally suspicious and wanted to protect her. I couldn't let her go alone.

I suppose that settled it then. We met at night by the art hut. There were ten of us, and two of them — Teresa and Jack, the leaders of the Midnight Club.

Teresa and Jack both came from families with a long tradition at Blackthorn. Their great, great grandparents had attended the school.

"Joining the Midnight Club is a privilege," Jack said to the group.

"We don't just let anybody in," Teresa agreed. "You must show us you're worthy."

I rolled my eyes.

"Every member before you had to pass the initiation," Teresa continued.

"Which is what?" I asked, irritation making me bold. It was cold and I was thinking about my cosy bed.

"We're about to get to that," Teresa snapped.

"It's just that we've been here for thirty minutes and all you've mentioned is how special the Midnight Club is and how great you are," I said.

January nudged me. "Please, stop," she whispered. I saw the tension on her face: she was afraid this opportunity would be taken from her. So, I held back.

"Your mission is to spend the night in Wilmore Mansion," said Jack.

There were rumbles in the group. We knew about Wilmore. There were photos of the ancient house displayed around the school. William Wilmore, who founded Blackthorn, used to live there and was said to haunt it.

"Listen up! These are your instructions. You must find a room in the mansion and stay there the entire night, by yourself, until morning. No one goes into that room except you," Jack explained.

Wilmore Mansion was a ten-minute walk from Blackthorn. The gate was riddled with overgrown shrubs and the long driveway had weeds pushing through the cracks.

We all approached and huddled outside, scared to enter. Then, of its own accord, the door swung open.

"Go on," commanded Teresa.

We shuffled inside. We entered a huge hall with cobwebs hanging like drapes. A few of us climbed the sweeping staircase. The rest split up to find a room downstairs.

I took the room next to January.

It's just one night, I told myself, standing in a dusty bedroom with a four-poster bed. *How hard could it be?*

I positioned myself under the window and waited the night out. January started singing and I was happy to hear her voice. But after a while she stopped. I assumed she had fallen asleep.

The night felt endless.

Finally, the sun came up. I jumped to my feet, ran out into the hall and burst into January's room ... but it was empty!

I sprinted down the hall, shouting her name. When the others realised what had happened, they sprang into action to look for January. We explored every room but no one could find her.

I had to raise the alarm. I felt sick as I ran back to school.

Teresa followed close behind and stopped me just as I reached the Headteacher's office. "Kacey!" she cried, breathless. "I heard about January. Talking to the Head might cause problems for the Club. I'm sure she's fine."

I narrowed my eyes at her. "Do you have some information that I don't?"

Teresa's eyes widened. "No! But at least let's have breakfast first and look later." She put her hand on my shoulder. "Trust me."

I was sure she knew something. "Whatever you know, tell me," I said, angrily. "If you don't, I'll call the police."

With a sigh and a nod, she led me outside and back to Wilmore Mansion.

We re-entered the ancient, dusty house and made our way back to January's room. Teresa ran her hand against the wall by the bed until a section gave way and swung open to reveal a second small room.

There was January, curled up in a ball in an old armchair.

"January!"
I exclaimed.
She looked
up, startled.

"She has so
much potential
that we extended
her initiation,"
Teresa explained.
"She has to
stay here for
one more night.
She agreed to
do it."

I turned to Teresa.
"It's not OK that
she's here alone
and nobody
knows where
she is!"

"I'm sorry," Teresa whispered before running away.

January and I walked back into the hall and sat on the sweeping staircase.

Finally, January spoke. "You were right about Teresa. I've come to the conclusion that secret societies are not for me!"

A letter from the Headteacher

Dear Students,

A recent incident involving a secret society has come to my attention. While Blackthorn Boarding School encourages extra-curricular activities, we do not condone anything that might put students in danger, or groups that are based on the exclusion of others.

May I remind all students that no one is allowed outside the school gates without a teacher or a permission slip. You are especially not allowed to enter private property. This is against the law and can lead to exclusion and a police investigation.

While we understand the long-standing history behind these societies, the safety of our students must come first. Therefore, we regret to inform you that two students have been expelled, and an internal investigation will be carried out.

Mr Basildon

Mr. Basildon

Headteacher, Blackthorn Boarding School

Youth Action for Change

Written by Samantha Montgomerie

A vision for change can be a powerful thing. Superheroes fight for justice in films. In real life, politicians and influential adults decide how we deal with big problems. But sometimes, passionate young people raise their voices and take action to make our world a better place. They make change happen.

Here are some of their stories.

Cleaning up our world's waters

Name:
Boyan Slat

Nationality:
Dutch

When he was 16 years old, Boyan Slat went on a scuba diving holiday in Greece. However, he was disappointed to see more plastic bags than fish in the sea. His first reaction was to ask: *Why can't we just clean this up?*

Boyan used his passion for science and building things to start to think of solutions. At school, he learnt how scientific devices could help clean up pollution in our world's waters. By the time he was 18, Boyan wanted to take action and build some equipment himself.

Boyan dropped out of university to create The Ocean Cleanup, an organisation with a mission to get rid of plastic from the world's waters. It focuses on places where the amount of plastic is at its worst, such as the Great Pacific Garbage Patch in the North Pacific.

Boyan used clever innovation to design a new system to fight ocean pollution. He invented 'interceptors', which use data and computers to find places with a high concentration of rubbish.

> The interceptors work in three steps:
> 1. A 600-metre-long 'floater skirt' makes a U-shape, acting like a wall in the water.
> 2. This wall and water currents work together like a funnel to collect plastic into a 'retention zone'.
> 3. This collection of plastic is taken to the shore to be recycled.

an ocean interceptor

Boyan wanted to stop rubbish from entering oceans in the first place, too. The interceptors also catch rubbish in rivers around the world that are most affected by plastic pollution. This makes sure that the rivers are clean before they reach the oceans.

Calling for education for all

Name:
Malala Yousafzai
(say: *Yoo-suf-z-eye*)

Nationality:
Pakistani

When Malala Yousafzai was 11 years old, she lost her right to an education. In 2007, a group called the Taliban invaded Pakistan, which led to schools for girls being closed. Violence and tensions grew due to the Taliban's rule. Malala and her family had to flee their home for safety.

In 2008, Malala gave her first speech: *How dare the Taliban take away my basic right to education?* at a local news club. The speech was a demonstration of her anger at the situation in her home country. It was shown on TV across Pakistan.

Malala began to share her thoughts on a blog for the BBC, which captured global attention. She used a fake name for protection. However, her real name did not stay hidden for long. On 9th October 2012, a Taliban gunman tracked her down and shot her on her school bus.

After months of recovery, Malala continued her fight until every girl in Pakistan could go to school. Many powerful people supported her, and Pakistan created its first Right to Education bill in 2012. This made education free and compulsory for all children aged 5 to 16.

At the age of 16, Malala spoke at the United Nations and declared that all children everywhere should have access to education. The United Nations named 12th July 'Malala Day' in recognition of her bravery and to highlight the struggle for education around the world.

Malala started the Malala Fund with her father to help give every girl the opportunity to learn and to choose her own future.

In 2014, Malala won the Nobel Peace Prize, making her the youngest winner at just 17 years old.

Malala speaking at the Transforming Education Summit at the United Nations in 2022.

Sparking a climate revolution

Name:
Greta Thunberg
(say: *toon-berg*)

Nationality:
Swedish

When Greta Thunberg first learnt about climate change, she felt angry that so little was being done to stop its impact. In August 2018, when she was 15, she used her frustration to take action. Instead of going to school, she made a large sign that said, 'School Strike for Climate'. She stood outside the Swedish parliament with her sign to get the attention of the nation's leaders. The Swedish press shared the story around the world.

Young people everywhere took inspiration from Greta's protest. Thousands joined her campaign, #FridaysforFuture, and around four million students skipped school on Fridays to take part in demonstrations for climate action.

Soon after she began her strikes, Greta got lots of invitations to speak about climate change. In 2019, she attended the Climate Action Summit in America.

To avoid flying to America and creating carbon pollution, she sailed across the Atlantic. Her speech: *How dare you?*, criticised world leaders for not doing enough to protect our planet. She inspired a generation to take a stand.

After leaving high school, Greta has continued to bring international attention to the impacts of climate change. Her actions have influenced public awareness and policies.

Greta Thunberg leading the Youth Strike 4 Climate rally through Bristol, UK, in 2020.

Leading the next generation

Name:
Thandiwe Abdullah
(say: *Than-dee-way*)

Nationality:
American

Thandiwe Abdullah grew up in a family of activists. She attended many Black Lives Matter meetings as a child, but soon realised that hardly any other children were there. When she was a teenager, she decided to create an organisation to help make safe spaces for young people to speak out against racism. She used her experience from the meetings and founded Black Lives Matter Youth Vanguard (say: *Van-gard*). This organisation works to start discussions and find solutions for a fair education system and society.

A key goal of Black Lives Matter is to combat racism and police violence. The Youth Vanguard organisation worked to reallocate money for school police departments to improve learning materials and conditions for students.

Thandiwe helped create the Black Lives Matter in Schools campaign, run by the National Education Association. The campaign encourages reflection, truthful conversations and impactful actions in schools to make sure that people of all races are treated fairly and equally.

When she was 14, Thandiwe joined the March for Our Lives demonstration and spoke passionately about the many young Black people who had lost their lives due to violence.

In 2018, she gave a speech to a crowd of 500,000 people at the Women's March in Los Angeles. An article named her one of the most influential teenagers of the year. Thandiwe has helped make sure that younger generations have a voice and a place to stand up for their rights.

Crowds at the 2018 Women's March in Los Angeles.

Inspiration for change

We can find solutions when we share a vision and fight for change. These influential young people show how bringing attention to problems can start conversations. Their determination to make a difference has led to positive results for all of us. They show how being brave and persevering can achieve great things. They demonstrate how we can stand up for what we believe in and take action for change – no matter how old or young we are.

A great ocean clean up

The Ocean Cleanup project focuses on collecting rubbish from the Great Pacific Garbage Patch. This is the largest of five plastic accumulation zones in our world's waters. It is around three times the size of France!

Winds and currents move the rubbish around, so the location and shape of the Great Pacific Garbage Patch are constantly changing. Computers help to target hotspots where there is a large build-up of rubbish.

Step 1:
Target plastic pollution by using computers and data.

Step 2:
Capture rubbish with 2.2-kilometre-long walls so that it floats into a retention zone.

Step 3:
Remove rubbish from the retention zone and onto a ship.

Step 4:
Recycle the plastics on shore.

Acknowledgements

The publishers gratefully acknowledge the permission granted to reproduce the copyright material in this book. Every effort has been made to trace copyright holders and to obtain their permission for the use of copyright material. The publishers will gladly receive any information enabling them to rectify any error or omission at the first opportunity.

p20 Allstar Picture Library Ltd/Alamy Stock Photo, p21 Ed Mulholland/Getty Images, pp56-57 vector illustration/Shutterstock, p60 1494/Shutterstock, p61 DPA picture alliance/Alamy Stock Photo, p63 Citizen of the Planet/Alamy Stock Photo, p64 Michael Scott/Alamy Stock Photo, p65 M7Studio/Shutterstock, p66 Enrique Shore/Alamy Stock Photo, p67 Stephen Chung/Alamy Stock Photo, pp68-69 1000 Words/Shutterstock, p70 Earl Gibson III/Shutterstock, p71 Lorna Roberts/Shutterstock, p72 ZUMA Press, Inc./Alamy Stock Photo, p73 RZ Images/Shutterstock, pp74-75 irin-k/Shutterstock, p74bl Citizen of the Planet/Alamy Stock Photo, p75t DPL/Alamy Stock Photo, p75bl Abaca Press/Alamy Stock Photo, p75br Connect Images/Alamy Stock Photo.

Published by Collins
An imprint of HarperCollins*Publishers*
The News Building, 1 London Bridge Street, London, SE1 9GF, UK

HarperCollins*Publishers*
Macken House, 39/40 Mayor Street Upper, Dublin 1, D01 C9W8, Ireland

Browse the complete Collins catalogue at
collins.co.uk

© HarperCollins*Publishers* Limited 2026

Wandle Learning Trust name and logo © Wandle Learning Trust

10 9 8 7 6 5 4 3 2 1

A catalogue record for this publication is available from the British Library.

ISBN 978-0-00-879101-8

All rights reserved. No part of this publication may be reproduced, stored in a retrieval system, or transmitted in any form by any means, electronic, mechanical, photocopying, recording or otherwise, without the prior written permission of the Publisher or a licence permitting restricted copying in the United Kingdom issued by the Copyright Licensing Agency Ltd, 5th Floor, Shackleton House, 4 Battle Bridge Lane, London SE1 2HX.

Without limiting the exclusive rights of any author, contributor or the publisher of this publication, any unauthorised use of this publication to train generative artificial intelligence (AI) technologies is expressly prohibited. HarperCollins also exercise their rights under Article 4(3) of the Digital Single Market Directive 2019/790 and expressly reserve this publication from the text and data mining exception.

Authors: Kereen Getten, Samantha Montgomerie and Oliver Sykes
Illustrators: Daniella Gyambibi-Peters (Illo Agency), Wan Norazura (Astound US) and Elijah Vardo
Publisher: Katie Sergeant
Product managers: Natasha Paul and Caroline Green
Education consultant: Charlotte Raby
Project manager: Emily Hooton
Phonics reviewers: Catherine Baker and Abbie Rushton
Proofreader and fact checker: Catherine Dakin
Cover designer: Sarah Finan
Cover images: Pheerasak Jomnuy/Shutterstock (front) and andreiuc88/Shutterstock (back)
Internal designer: 2Hoots Publishing Services Ltd
Production controller: Sophie Waeland

Developed in collaboration with Wandle Learning Trust

Printed in the UK by Martins the Printers

Made with responsibly sourced paper and vegetable ink

Scan to see how we are reducing our environmental impact.

Collins would like to thank Abi Rothe, Nicola Dickens and the schools involved in the Code pilot for contributing to the development of this book.

Access the planning and resources to teach this book at littlewandlecode.org.uk